Evidence of Elephants

This Poem Doesn't Rhyme (Ed.)
Does W Trouble You? (Ed.)
The Magnificent Callisto

Evidence of Elephants

Poems by Gerard Benson

Illustrated by Alison Forsythe

VIKING

This book is for
Eleanor and Heidi Young,
and Miranda Clearbury

VIKING

Published by the Penguin Group
Penguin Books Ltd, 27 Wrights Lane, London W8 5TZ, England
Penguin Books USA Inc., 375 Hudson Street, New York, New York 10014, USA
Penguin Books Australia Ltd, Ringwood, Victoria, Australia
Penguin Books Canada Ltd, 10 Alcorn Avenue, Toronto, Ontario, Canada M4V 3B2
Penguin Books (NZ) Ltd, 182–190 Wairau Road, Auckland 10, New Zealand

Penguin Books Ltd, Registered Offices: Harmondsworth, Middlesex, England

First published 1995
1 3 5 7 9 10 8 6 4 2

Filmset in Linotron Palatino
by Rowland Phototypesetting Ltd, Bury St Edmunds, Suffolk

Printed in Great Britain by Butler & Tanner Ltd, Frome and London

A CIP catalogue record for this book is available from the British Library

ISBN 0–670–85960–5

Contents

This Poem

*T*his poem, which is about itself,
Is confident that it must be
The very best poem on the subject,
If only because there are no others.

All the same, this poem is nervous,
Never having tried this before;
And extremely aware that . . . that there is . . .
That it has no second chance.

Any other poem which is about itself
Will not be about this poem;
And any other poem about this poem
Will not be about itself.

You will find this poem difficult to read
If you hold it up to a mirror;
And that is the only way
This poem can get a view of itself.

If at present you are not interested
In this poem, it will bide its time;
But it will do almost anything
To catch your attention: even suddenly rhyme.

As the author of this poem
I can choose when to end it;
But the poem itself
Does not know when it will end.

River Song

'*O*h where are you going?' said Rover to river,
'You flow always downward. Why should that be?'
'I gather the droplets of water together
And carry them home to their mother, the sea.'

'From moment to moment,' said Rover to river,
'Your waters are changing, yet you stay the same.'
'No. I am the mocker of every map-maker;
Although they outline me and give me a name.'

'I'm banked and I'm bridged,' said river to Rover.
'I'm built by; I'm fished in, I'm wished on as well.
But I am a winder; I love to wander.
Every day I am different, with stories to tell,'

'Of floods and disasters,' said river to Rover,
'Of long lazy summers, of ducks in my weeds,
Of wild otter huntings, of strange ghostly hauntings,
Of crisp frozen winters with ice on my reeds.'

'Of towns that surround me,' said river to Rover,
'Until I escape through the bridges, to fields
Where brown cattle wallow beside my green willows,
And small beetles strut, with their bright shining
  shields.'

'And all the time downward,' said river to Rover,
'I travel past building and boulder and tree.
I gather the driplets and droplets together
And hurry them home to their mother, the sea.'

On the Rock Face

Stepping out
Gingerly placing my boot
Onto a tiny hold,
The fossilized thumbnail perhaps
Of a pre-Jurassic child,
I shift my weight
Clumsily, delicately a foot
To the left.
  Breathe.
   Air is beautiful.
Trusting my bulk
To the fingerprint
On the middle finger
Of my right hand
I edge further west.
  Again breathe.
  Like rare wine.

Soon
It will be time to rise,
Hoist my midriff
Inches up and back.
   Breathe.
   Air is strength.
Now left hand will stretch
And reach
And claw
The tiny jutting triangle of rock
Which is my horizon.
   Swing out.
   And breathe!

Craig-yr-Deryn

Clinging to igneous rock
Hundreds of feet up, my blood
Racing, heart thumping, I scratch
For a stronger handhold.
A crow soars below me.

Right foot is wedged
Into an imaginary crack,
The left rests on air,
Knee jammed fiercely
Sideways into the rock face.

The wind whisks past me
And my hands are cold.
Up and down, both are impossible.
I shall be here always.
There is nowhere for me to go.

*Note: Craig-yr-Deryn is the name of a huge
rock in North Wales.*

Time is Eating the Cliffs

*T*ime is eating the cliffs,
Slowly digesting them.

Come snow, come rain,
High tide and low,

Grain after grain,
Come breeze, come gale,

Come ice, come sun,
Time is eating the cliffs.

For a small while
Time will allow

Grasses to grow
In cracks of the cliffs,

Flowers to show
Their bright brave faces,

And will slyly reveal
The ancient hieroglyphs,

The curves and spirals,
The tough, ridged braille

Of ammonites, belemnites
Entombed aeons ago –

Fossil remains
To remind you of this:

That day by day,
Bite by tiny bite,

Time, who made the cliffs,
Is eating them away.

A Small Star

I live on a small star
Which it is my job to look after;
It whirls through space
Wrapped in a cloak of water.

It is a wonderful star:
Wherever you look there is life,
Though it's held at either end
In a white fist of ice.

There are creatures that move
Through air, sea and earth,
And growing things everywhere
Make beauty from dirt.

Everything is alive!
Even the very stones:
Amazing crystals grow
Deep under the ground.

And all the things belong,
Each one to the other.
I live on a precious star
Which it is my job to look after.

I am Taken from Earth

I am taken from earth and wrung from rock.
Rounds are locked together.
Stiff-hard I am, yet I twine and twist.
Heavy I am for the prisoner
Yet I am light for the lovely lady,
Who treasures me and places me close to her heart.
By me are kingdoms ruled.
By me are wooden towns
Held on the water's surface.
I am known to both dog and bear.
I am no stronger than my frailest part.

  Name my name.

A Transparent Riddle

Dug from the desert, I was tormented with heat.
Then I was cut and ground and polished.
Without witchcraft I can alter your size.
Working with my brother I carry things closer.
I was framed, folded and placed in a hinged coffin.
    If you know me, name me.

Bei-shung

I am *Bei-shung*, they call me the white bear.
I am the hidden king of these bamboo forests,
Invisible with my white fur and my black fur
Among this snow, these dark rocks and shadows.

I am the hidden king of these mountain heights,
Not a clown, not a toy. I do not care
To be seen. I walk, for all my weight,
Like a ghost on the soles of my black feet.

Invisible with my black fur and my white fur
I haunt the streams. I flip out little fishes;
I scoop them out of the water with my hand.
(I have a thumb, like you. I have a hand.)

Among this sparkling snow, these rocks and shadows,
I roam. Time is my own. My teeth are massive.
My jaw is a powerful grinder. I feed
On chewy bamboo, on small creatures, fish, birds.

You call me Panda. I am King *Bei-shung*.

In a Kenyan Garden

A lizard, dinosaur in miniature,
Blue as a cornflower, stands sentry on the path.
Mousebirds run in the trees, peep between branches,
Or swing like big commas on the telegraph wires.

Taller than any man, the massive leaves
Of a banana tree droop and begin to rot.
The rains have come and autumn has begun
But this afternoon the garden is a slow oven.

Like a small golden harlequin or highwayman,
A black-masked weaver bird watches me while I write,
Then flies to the banana tree and delicately begins
To tease away one fibre with his beak.

He braces against his legs and twists and tugs
Till he has freed a twelve inch length,
Flits to his village tree and cleanly threads
The new strand into the round dome of his nest.

All the hot afternoon he works, stripping the leaf,
Crafting through miraculous knowledge a perfect
    sphere,
One nest among a hundred on that tree,
Where, when the sun has disappeared, he'll rest.

Evidence of Elephants

If you had had just the bones to go on,
    Only the bones,
Could you have guessed an elephant?
    How could you know?

Oh, you could work out the size and so on
    By measuring the bones,
But the vast flapping ears, that caked-mud grey,
    They would not show.

Nor the trunk. From the skull you'd never guess
    At that long swinging trunk,
Boneless and flexible, sensitive and beautiful,
    Hanging in front,

Or lifted to blare like a trumpet, or to caress
    Another elephant.
If I had only the bones to help me,
    I think I'd be stumped.

The Scholar's Cat

*P*angur, my white cat, and I,
We each a different skill apply;
His art is all in hunting mice,
Mine is in thought, deep and precise.

My greatest joy is just to sit
And con my page with subtle wit;
While Pangur Ban will frisk and play
Nor envy me my quieter way.

We are companions, never bored
In our small house, in true accord
We test our faculties, and find
Some occupation for the mind.

He, by his arts, can trap and kill
A hapless mouse with perfect skill.
And I, after much careful gleaning
Can bring to light a hidden meaning.

His eye, as keen as any sword,
Is focused on the skirting board;
While I direct my milder looks
Upon the knowledge in my books.

When he pursues a mouse with speed,
Pangur rejoices in the deed;
I exult when in the brain
Some knotty point at last comes plain.

Though we are always thus together,
We neither one obstruct the other;
Pangur and I pursue alone
Two separate arts, to each his own.

His curious work is his delight,
Which he rehearses day and night;
And daily I bring clarity
Where there had been obscurity.

Note: This is a translation of a ninth-century Irish poem, the first ever to mention the domestic cat.

Minoushka

The leaves swirl in the wind,
Yellow and gold and brown:
And, brown and gold, Minou
Hunts them up and down,
A tiny frisking clown.

A whisking, frisking scrap,
She bends in the afternoon sun.
She tumbles after her leaf,
Choosing a particular one:
Pounce! and the game is done.

Then she slinks, a minute panther,
The leaf gripped in her jaws,
Across the October grass,
To fetch her trophy indoors
Padding on delicate paws.

Dog at the Temple

*P*aws crossed, an exhausted dog
Sprawls in the shadow
Of a stone pillar
Carved with gesturing gods.

His ribs rise and fall.
His tongue lolls.
Flank and jowl
Lie flat to the ground.

The picture-words stand in columns.
Straightbacked to outface Time
Beast and bird-headed gods
Hold beautiful postures.

Here in Dendera Temple,
Where the sky goddess
Daily gives birth to the sun,
Queen Cleopatra prayed.

Now foreign tourists
In hats and knee-length shorts
Genuflect with cameras.
Robed beggars lurk.

Tour-guides recite their lessons
Standing beside stones
That have heard the voice
Of Cleopatra.

.   .   .

An hour has passed.
The dog has not moved.

Hedgehog on the Lawn

Strange. There is a hedgehog snouting
under the plantains on my neighbour's grass,
the first I ever saw by daylight;
her prickly back is speckled like a thrush's breast.

Her long face is foxish, not hog-like,
a triangle bevelled to a small sensitive nose.
She does not fear me, even trots toward me.
This daytime feeding is wrong. Is it day-hunger?

I am not the only watcher. Elliott is here too,
the big black cat. He sits well away from her.
His huge yellow eyes shine in the shadows.
Is he remembering a paw full of spikes?

One minute she is there, the next not;
like a conjuring trick she vanishes among
the friendly weeds under my neighbour's bushes;
and as for Elliott, it is me he is watching now.

Yum!

I like pepper on my ice cream;
  Some like ice cream chilly.
I put ice cubes in the tea pot;
  Boiling tea is silly.

If you want your bread to harden,
  (Hard enough to chew)
Mix the flour with best cement
  And butter it with glue.

Some folks think this poem's stupid;
  Others think they're wrong.
Set it to a little tune
  And sing it as a song.

Lim

*T*here once was a bard of Hong Kong
Who thought limericks were too long.

Sir Bert

*T*here once was a knight, called Sir Bert,
Who said: 'Oh, this armour *does* hurt!
    I can stand it no more;
    Nip down to the store
And fetch me a non-iron shirt.'

The Poet from Lyme

*T*here once was a poet from Lyme,
Who could not get his poems to rhyme.
 Whatever he did,
 They just didn't work.
He should have used a rhyming dictionary.

April

*A*pril Thackeray
The music teacher's daughter
Had eyes like skies
And hands like water.
She wore a shirt
Of daffodil yellow,
And we played duets
On her Pa's piano.

We never went out.
The simple fact is,
We only met
To play or practise,
And though I imagined
Walking beside her,
The gap between us
Could not have been wider.

April Thackeray
Was nobody's fool.
We shared the wide
Piano stool:
'One . . . and . . . two,'
She'd lead, I'd follow,
When we played together
On her Pa's piano.

Blue Jeans and Silver Guitars

*T*he singer sang honeyed words,
  'Your eyes are dreaming!'
And heard the pressed-together girls
  Sighing and screaming.

When he thrashed the tightened strings
  Of his silver guitar
The excited electric sounds
  Throbbed to a star.

The star with the speed of a dream
  Flew to the eyes
Of a listening girl, who became
  Suddenly wise.

With the knowledge of a million years
  She danced in each limb;
The singer saw her star-lit eyes
  Looking at him;

Two eyes that were fed with his words
  In all that crowd
Of pretty, blue-jeaned, swaying girls
  Sang out aloud!

.   .   .

The singer sang truthful words,
  'There are stars in your eyes!'
And heard the pressed-together girls,
  Their screams, their sighs.

Speeches of Kings and Shepherds

*T*hree kings we be,
And from afar,
And through the shivering cold,
We have travelled
On horse and camel,
Guided by a star;
And we have brought the baby
Presents three,
Incense and myrrh and gold.
And here in this rough place
We kneel, to look upon his face,
And give our presents, one two three.

Shepherds are we
And from the field
Where, by our simple fire
We sat,
At chat of this and that,
Sent by an angel choir
Have we come here on foot,
To greet the child
With gifts – a fleece, a flute,
Warmth for the babe and music sweet;
And now we lay them at his feet.
Look! The baby smiled.

In Hospital

My tongue is mute.
The words are locked
Inside my head.
Beside my bed
A bowl of fruit,
And you who smile
And talk to me
And hold my hand,
I knew you in
Another time.
I know you still
But cannot speak.
My tongue is dead.
The words are shut
Inside my head.

Fishing

*T*here is a fine
line

between fishing
and standing
on the bank
like an idiot.

Goal!

*I*t's Dicky to Dirty,
And Dirty back to Dicky . . .
He swerves past three men
    (Oh, he's tricky)
And he lofts the ball
Into the middle,
A pin-point pass,
    Which finds Diddle;
Diddle back-heels
(Very neat, that, clever!)
And lays it in the path
    Of Trevor,
Our six million pound
Striker (well 25 pee
If you want the truth)
    And he
Drives it, right-footed;
It strikes the bar
And rebounds into the path
    Of Pa
(Our oldest player)
But unluckily it hits
His walking stick . . .
    He sits
Suddenly, and the ball
Trickles back to Trevor,
Who shoots!! Unstoppable!!!
    Did you ever!?!?

Their goalie palms
It away but straight
To Dozy (who's asleep) . . .
   But wait . . . !
Patch has got the ball
(He's half collie –
Recently signed from Rovers)
   And, golly!
He's nose down, tail up –
He's running rings
Round a sheepish defence –
   He brings
The leather to the educated feet
Of Gerard* (You bet!)
Now one neat flick and it's
   In the Net!

* Note: Or, if you wish, put in your own
name as a late substitute.

Humpty-Dumpty Remembers

I got so tired of that wall,
   just sitting there day after day.
No life for an educated egg,
   an egg with something to say.
      No way. No way.

To the right the Palace and the stables,
   to the left a small hill, my wall
And miles and miles of dull countryside.
   Nothing to look at at all.
      It was bound to pall.

I was supposed to be the lookout.
   Oh what a boring game.
There was nothing whatever to watch;
   absolutely nobody came.
      It was always the same.

The Palace was made of plywood;
   there was nothing in it to steal.
We hadn't an enemy in the world –
   the place wasn't even real.
      How would you feel?

Just sitting there while the Duke
　　marched his ten thousand men
Up to the top of the hill,
　　counted up to ten, then
　　　　Marched them down again?

I tell you, I was bored – just bored.
　　I wasn't pushed. I didn't fall.
One fine day I thought for a lark
　　I'd jump off the stupid wall.
　　　　That was all.

Then they rushed the foot-soldiers
　　down the hill, the cavalry too,
With half a mile of sellotape
　　and a blooming great tube of glue.
　　　　But what could they do?

I thought I'd scrambled it for them
　　(you'll pardon my little yolk!)
But they got a new unbreakable Humpty,
　　(it's enough to make a chap choke),
　　　　Stuffed, poor bloke.

The Magic Potion

*T*here once was a wizard so cunning and wise
That if he should chance to run out of supplies
He could make up his spells from whatever he'd got,
For instance, no ratsbane? he'd use a shallot!
Or in seasons when worm-juice was not to be found
He would make do with slugs, which he bought by the
    pound
And kept in the fridge with his salad and eggs
And his famous collection of centipedes' legs.

If you wanted a potion to magic your teacher
To a toad or an asp or some other dear creature
You had only to ask him and pay him in cash
(For he wouldn't take cheques and thought credit
    cards trash)
And as soon as he'd heard you (and counted the
    money)
He'd be mixing the wasp brains and turnip flower
    honey,
Or, if he'd run out of them, bull's-eyes and cheese,
Or pig's tears and glue, if he couldn't get these.

He was brewing one day, I was helping the man
(For I like to be helpful whenever I can),
When he paused as he stirred with the long copper
    spoon:
'Tut! I need some shark's blood or some moss from the
    moon,
Or I could just make do I suppose' (here he smiled)
'With a hair from the head of a Really Good Child,
If such could be found.' 'Why that's easy!' I cried,
'You can have one of mine.' 'Why, of course,' he
    replied.

Then he muttered some words as he thickened the
    brew,
'Zooks, Abracadabra! I think this should do.
Perhaps I should test it. It does smell delicious.
And if it's all right, I will grant you three wishes.'
And he took just a lick, and before you could say,
'Hey Presto!' the wizard had vanished away.
He has not been seen since, though I've searched hard
    and long.
Now how in the world did that potion go wrong?

Riddle-Me-Right

Card magic is mighty easy to me, so are legerdemain and mesmerisM
Outlandish are my powers and my personality and my paraphernaliA
Nothing is to me impossible. No, nothing. Absolutely no thinG
Just try and explain my flashy, trashy, trumpery tricks. Try! I
Usually defy all measly, mundane explanations. Mysterious magiC
Rodomontade is my reason, my rhetoric, my rationale, my trade. I
Excel at deception, at disappearance, at inducing doubt. Am I A
?Riddling mountebank, dear reader, or a miraculous master magiciaN?
?   ?

48

The Witch Griselle

Oh see Griselle, the riding witch,
Her gnarled and twisted fingers twitch
Upon the whippy hazel switch
Wherewith she slashes at the thighs
Of Nag, her broomstick horse, who plies
His course across the tumbled skies.

      Her laugh, like quarrelling rooks
      Crows out, while ancient books
Of spells fly flapping round her eerie steed.
      Her eyes, like smouldering coals
      Glare at the mystic scrolls
Of symbols that no other eye may read.

She rides astride, Griselle the witch,
A snorting horse as black as pitch
And weaves a spell with silken stitch,
Twisting between the stars her threads
While sleepers writhe in nightmare beds
As gnomes and devils din their heads.

      But at the dawn's first light
      She vanishes from sight;
A kind old village dame in specs and shawl
      Who sips a dish of tea
      Is all that you will see.
But look – her broom is tethered to the wall.

A Tale of Two Citizens

I have a Russian friend who lives in Minsk
And wears a lofty hat of beaver skinsk,
(Which does not suit a man so tall and thinsk).
He has a frizzly beard upon his chinsk.
He keeps his britches up with safety pinsk.
  'They're so much better than those thingsk
  Called belts and bracekies, don't you thinksk?'
  You'll hear him say, the man from Minsk.

He has a Polish pal who's from Gdansk,
Who lives by selling drinksks to football fansk,
And cheese rolls, from a little caravansk.
(He finds it pleasanter than robbing banksk).
He also uses pinsk to hold his pantsk.
  'Keep up one's pantsk with rubber bandsk!?
  It can't be donesk! It simply can'tsk!
  Not in Gdansk!' he'll say. 'No thanksk!'

They're so alikesk that strangers often thinksk
That they are brothers, yesk, or even twinsk.
'I live in Minsk but I was born in Omsk,'
Says one. His friend replies, 'That's where *I'm* fromsk!
Perhapsk we're brothers after all, not friendsk.'
  So they wrote homesk and asked their Mumsk
  But found they weren'tsk; so they shook handsk
  And left for Minsk, and for Gdansk.

Tattoo Blues

I'm a sight! I'm a sight! I'm a sight!
I'm enough to give old Frankenstein a fright!
When I started this tattooing lark I thought of it as Art,
And I chose a pretty rosebud and a neatly arrowed
   heart;
If only I had stuck to that, I might have been all right,
   But I didn't, so I ended up a sight!

I'm a mess! I'm a mess! I'm a mess!
   I'm enough to scare the monster in Loch Ness!
I thought I'd have my pectorals as purple porcupines
Then the habit really got me and I'm covered with
   designs:
I've a warthog on one forearm, a hyena on the other,
Plus a large two-headed dragon with a caption reading
   'Mother'.
I've a spider's web across my face, a hornet on my
   neck,
While all across my bottom there's a shark-infested
   wreck,
And round my waist some creature that you'd never
   even guess.
   I'm a mess! I'm a mess! I'm a mess!

Trombone Man
(for Kid)

*H*e played upon the sad trombone,
The sad trombone, the sad trombone.
A minor tune of tender tone
He played upon the sad trombone,
From which a purple flower grew
Whene'er he blew, whene'er he blew;
And streams of bulging bubbles, too,
Which floated far above the town
And never burst, nor wandered down;
Or melting chocolate would pour
Its sweetness on the dancing floor,
Where rocking stompers swung and grooved,
And rhythmed as the music moved.

And while he played the sad trombone,
And slid the slider in and out,
I heard a prancing dancer shout:
'Oh look, how back and forth he slides
That slider; see the way it glides
Under the lights, so golden yellow,
And hear the music, dark and mellow
That billows from the sad trombone.'

And then the prooping sousaphone
Began; the wriggling clarionet,
The drumskin and the bright trum-pet,
Slap-happy bass and tall pi-anner,
All joined the song in stately manner,
Adding a sweep of harmony
To that unrolling melody.

Each line of music, soft or loud,
Spoke sadness to that dancing crowd,
But most of all, the wailful moan
Of him who blew the sad trombone,
His head thrown back, his cheeks outblown,
The eyes of one who thinks alone,
His thumping two-tone shoes emphatic,
His stance, his pumping arm dramatic,
As with his breath he coaxed along
Through puckered lips that minor song,
Upon that sad, that sad trombone!
That glad trombone, that mad trombone.
The sad trombone, the sad trombone,
The sad, the mad, the glad
Trom-
      bone.
         Yeah.

The Inventor's Advertisement

*P*rofessor de Brayno, Inventor-at-Large
Will invent what you need at a very small charge.
Just give me a ring or a personal call;
No job is too large – and no job is too small.

To show you my skill at this neatest of crafts,
I've invented a cat-flap that keeps out all draughts
(Though it does admit chessmen, I'm working on that,
And I still haven't solved one last problem – the cat
Refuses to use it!) However, it looks
Very splendid indeed! I've a telly that cooks,
With a channel for beans and another for jelly
(Which is more than you get with your average telly).
I've a one-leggèd table, a two-leggèd stool
And a marvellous three-leggèd desk for your school.
I've invented a shirt with retractable sleeves
And a burglar alarm that can recognize thieves,
And odourless trainers, and non-falling socks,
And self-winding ear-rings (they're 10 pee a box).
I've a bicycle wheel with invisible spokes,
A Gigglecomputer that makes up new jokes,
A silent alarm clock that saves you from waking
And some edible glue that stops jelly from shaking.

I've inventions for this and inventions for that,
So if you're in need, and would like a brief chat,
Just pick up your phone now and give me a ring;
My number is . . . dash it! . . . oh bother the thing!
I've forgotten my number! I know what we'll do!
If you need some Inventing, why *I will ring you!!*

Whispers in the Wood

Did you not see me when you came into the wood?
Did you not? You didn't see me at all?
I wasn't hiding. I was watching for you.
Did you notice the colour of the dry stone wall
Shift from goose-grey to buttery? Didn't you at all?

You say it often does that. Yes. And I'm usually there.
But perhaps, instead, you heard me? Surely you
    heard?
Nothing? You heard nothing? The wood went
    suddenly silent?
That was me. The trill of an unknown bird
Through the copse? It could have been me you heard.

Did you notice a spider web that billowed like a sail?
Were you not visited by an unexpected thought
About someone who may have lived in this wood
At some time in the past? Were you caught
Unawares? Were you sad? . . . I was that thought.

I have been watching for you, and waiting.
You like this wood. So do I. I know you well.
You do not see me but I'm not far away.
When you come here to play, do you not catch a smell
Sometimes in autumn? Do you never sense my
    presence? Well . . . ?

Poem for the Changing of the Clocks

This hour
  in the night
    When I wait
      in the dark
        bedroom
          for sleep to take me away
      Passes with tick
      and tock
        of the wooden clock,
And I hear also
  in my imagination
    The silent breathing
      in   out
      in   out
Of a thousand other
  listeners to the night.
Cats stalk the slates
On firm and soundless feet
And tear the darkness with their yowls.
The joists and timbers
  stretch and sigh,
Ghosts in the attic creak.
  And dew beads the listening sycamore
That inks the space
  between me and the indifferent moon.

And this is the hour, perhaps
That will never be,
That will be looped into time
As the clocks of England
Adjust after their long summer
    To the rigours of Greenwich.

A child turns in its sleep
And somewhere an aged tap
    drips
            and
                drips.

Who Lived Here?

Who lived here in this house
  In the middle of the wood,
Where bushes now and creepers grow,
  And the soft fungus? Who could?

This overgrown gap was once a door
  And the floor has rotted away;
Birds and insects busy themselves
  Where children used to play.

Who lived here in this house?
  Who slept in this rusty bed?
Who papered these broken walls?
  Are they all dead?

Where there used to be stairs
  Stands a tall birch tree;
The roof has fallen, the grate
  Is black, the windows empty.

An owl roosts on the last beam;
  In a drainpipe sleeps a mouse.
But I sense the ghosts of long ago.
  Who lived here? In this house?

Spot the Difference

*T*he two pictures look very much alike.
In both a boy is diving into a swimming pool.
A girl sits, dangling her feet in the water.
A nice woman in a flowery frock
Is pointing at something we cannot see.
And a faithful dog I have nicknamed 'Soldier'
Is standing guard over a tennis ball.
There is a table laid for a picnic tea.

I am spotting the differences. There should be ten.
Look. There's no logo on the second boy's trunks,
And the second girl has only one hair ribbon.
And mummy number two – her watch has gone.
I don't like it. The bird has flown from the sky,
There's an extra cloud on the horizon,
And the swimming pool ladder has lost some rungs.
(That's six.) Oh, and Soldier has only one eye.

Who has done this to these nice people?
Look. They've got no milk for their tea;
Their jug has disappeared. Somebody hates them –
There are only three legs to their picnic table.
Which leaves me with just one to get.
(And to think I thought both pictures the same!)
Got it! Where mummy is pointing – there in the
    shrubbery –
Among those badly drawn leaves, isn't that

The muzzle of a rifle? And who is it pointing at?

The Football Ghosts

*A*t night, when the stadium is empty,
When the grass in the moonlight is silver-grey,
When the goals look like hungry fishing nets,
   It is then the old ghosts play.

When all the crisp packets and fag-ends
And the drink cans have been swept up,
And the crowd has left, and the gates are locked,
   They play for the Phantom Cup.

Thin clouds drift across the face of the moon,
The grass stirs, a preeping whistle sounds,
And silent invisible spectators
   Throng the deserted stands.

And twenty-two ghosts in long-legged shorts
Dance the ball across the silvered grass,
A ball you can almost see, the old game –
   Run, dribble and pass.

Pale shades and shadows, heroes of bygone days,
Under the gaze of the moon, sidestep and swerve,
And crowds silently cheer as the ball floats
   Goalwards in an unseen curve.

Ghost Writing

*I*n the depths of the sea
a skeletal hand –
a white crab
clings to an iron bulkhead
then feels its way
in the ocean's darkness
sideways
like a ghost writing
on that decaying steel
a silent message.

This was the *Titanic*
and where it lies
there is still a little life
among the shoes,
the suitcases, the plates,
the cast-iron toilets –
a rattail fish and
a dead-white hand
which moves sideways making
invisible graffiti.

Waiting for the Stones to Hatch

Close to the horizon the sea is black; the sky
Is weighted with cloud. Low over the water
Strung like a dark necklace, a flight
Of cormorants hurries into the wind.
Waves reach breaking point in a travelling
Quarrel of white foam. Stones on the shore
Spell a long story – a history of the world;
Grey pebbles, grey sky, grey waters.
   Rain speckles the stones, earth eggs of amazing
Density, whose hatching we await with scared
Patience. The cormorants are out of sight
Beyond the spit. The horizon has disappeared.
Among the blue-grey pebbles I can see
Red ellipses, lumps of white quartz.

Postcards in 23 Words

Postcard from Fairyland

*S*pell-binding scenery.
Lots of moonbathing,
(no tan).
Food delicious,
portions small.
Elves quarrelsome.
Was granted three wishes –
messed it up.
So home Thursday.

Postcard from Anywhere

I lie in bed
quite without fear,
play in the sand,
swim by the pier.
Having a wonderful time.
Glad you're not here.

Postcard from the North Pole

*S*urrounded by icy whiteness.
It is winter, and always nighttime.
The stars twinkle forever.
But I miss you all –
and home –
and sunlight.

Postcard from Three-Bear Cottage

*N*ot much of a holiday.
The furniture is broken.
Daddy Bear booms all the time –
Baby Bear squeaks.
Nothing to eat but porridge.

My Valentine

(written on a computer with a spell check)

I think I'm in HOVE,
(Or might it be LOVE?)
I certainly LICK
You a lot (or KICK
You perhaps, who NOSE?)
Your sweet little KNOWS
Like the bud of a ROPE,
It makes my HART LOPE
Like a JACK-in-a-BOG,
And your pretty new FROG
With its ribbons and BONES
And your bracelet of STAINS
SOOT you ever so fine,
So I PREY you'll be mine,
Be my sweet VALETUDINARIAN.

GEARED BENISON

To Catch an Elephant

*R*equires patience and attention to detail
But any girl or boy should be able
To master this method; it's quite simple.
Physical strength is not necessary
Nor is specialized knowledge;
But you will require quick thinking, courage,
A few simple skills – and of course luck.
(If you are not a lucky person
Do not even consider it, but purchase
Your elephant from a reputable dealer).

You will need: some buns, a step-ladder,
Binoculars, blackboard and chalk, tweezers,
A match box,* and (unless you are already there)
A ticket to India or Africa.
Use can also be found for a small table
Not to mention a good barrier cream and a sun hat.

* *Note: For African elephants you should use the larger 'kitchen-size' match box.*

Right! Display the buns on the table.
On the blackboard write in large letters:
FREE BUNS!   JUMBO OFFER!
Having done so, climb up the ladder
(Which should be placed in the cover
Of a bombax tree) and wait.
The binoculars may be used to scan the horizon
(Which is usually to be found some distance away,
Where the sky and the earth meet).
Elephants will eventually emanate.
Keep very still. This is the crucial moment.
The herd will approach, attracted by your notice.

While they are choosing their buns
You should be choosing your elephant.
(Plump for one with a nice flexible trunk
And well-spaced ears). Now, when your elephant
Is picking up its bun (you could use cup cakes)
It will be momentarily distracted.
This is the time for action.
With a practised flick of the wrist,
Quickly reverse the binoculars
And look through them at your selected elephant.
Grasp it firmly with the tweezers,
Lift gently and place in the match box
(Which should have been lined with cotton wool).

The Invention

*A*t first it was just an idea
(As a matter of fact, a dream).
I woke up not exactly seeing it
But knowing it could be.

Then it was a question of trying things,
Glue, elastic bands, clockwork motors,
A chopstick and a magnet, a needle,
The heel of a boot, a washing-up bowl.

The problem started in the mind
But soon turned itself into *things*,
My clumsiness caused difficulties,
But I kept on. I kept on and on.

Once I had drawn it, it got easier;
And the man at the garage helped
When he gave me some old scrap.
'Scrap' he called it! If only he knew!

And now here it is. I made it and it works
(Not quite the same as the dream)
And I am going to make another one,
Only better – and easier to construct.

Gorse

Gorse is a trumpet song.
　It spikes out of the earth,
　　A welcome pain.

It will spear your hands.
　It will wound your skin,
　　Bead you with scarlet.

It is 'I am' in all seasons.
　It blares its trumpet song
　　Tan-ta-ra to the skies.

It is a still fire.
　Yellow on the hillsides,
　　Coldly burning.

Fog Ice

*T*he thousand leaves of the bushes
are thorned with ice.
Minute splinters
serry the leaf edges,
sharp, gleaming, like barbaric

jewellery, intricately bright.
Every stem white;
each branch brilliant,
drawn upcurving against
dark houses, the loaded sky.

Grace and beauty – silversmith's work,
but cold as fear.
Filigree ferns,
tall beeches are sugared
sculpture. Tiny glass daggers

protect rose petals; oaks display
their skeletons,
white in the murk.
Words float in the chill air,
writhing shapes of mist in mist.

After the Book is Closed

Whether it is the words
   or their meanings,
Or the sounds they make,
   or the way they echo one another;
Or simply the pictures
   they paint in the imagination,
Or the ideas they begin,
   or their rhythms . . .

Whether it is the words
   or their histories,
Their curious journeys
   from one language to the next;
Or simply the shapes they make
   in the mouth –
Tongue and lips moving,
   breath flowing . . .

Whether it is the words
   or the letters used
To spell them, the patterns
   they make on the page;
Or simply the way they call feelings
   into the open
Like a fox seen suddenly in a field
   from a hurrying train . . .

Whether it is the words
   or the spaces between –
The white silences
   among the dark print,
I do not know.
   But I know this: that a poem
Will sing in my mind
   long after the book is closed.

Index of First Lines